Clarence Thomas Urmy, William Doxey, John Henry Nash

A vintage of verse

Clarence Thomas Urmy, William Doxey, John Henry Nash

A vintage of verse

ISBN/EAN: 9783743383388

Manufactured in Europe, USA, Canada, Australia, Japa

Cover: Foto ©Andreas Hilbeck / pixelio.de

Manufactured and distributed by brebook publishing software
(www.brebook.com)

Clarence Thomas Urmy, William Doxey, John Henry Nash

A vintage of verse

A VINTAGE OF VERSE

BY

CLARENCE URMY

AUTHOR OF

" A ROSARY OF RHYME "

WILLIAM DOXEY

AT THE SIGN OF THE LARK

SAN FRANCISCO

1897

Five hundred copies printed

The Doxey Press

TO MABEL

So one in heart and thought, I trow,
That thou mightst press the strings and
    I might draw the bow,
And both would meet in music sweet,
Thou and I, I trow.
—SIDNEY LANIER.

CONTENTS

CONTENTS

CONTENTS

CONTENTS

FROM VINE-CLAD HILLS

THE GOLDEN GATE

WAVE-WASHED by that quiescent sea
Balboa sighted rapturously,
And fanned by winds replete with lore
From Orient and Arctic shore,
It stands, a door unique and quaint,
Saint Francis for its patron saint—
The open sesame to bowers
Of far-famed sunshine, fruit, and flowers,
The portal to a wide expanse
Whose very name exhales romance.

From north, from south, a streamlet flows
From sheltered vales of vine and rose;
While larger rivers gleaming stray
Through golden wheat-fields to the bay;
Broad pathways lead to land of pine,
Or land where orange-boughs entwine;

To slopes where grape and olive grow,
Or far heights of eternal snow —
A country peerless, wondrous, great,
And guarded by a golden gate.

When Twilight, Eve's fond alchemist,
Weaves arabesques in amethyst,
The land about the gateway teems
With shadows, reveries, and dreams —
The phantom shadows of white sails
Blown hitherward by halcyon gales —
The dulcet reveries that throng
With Mission bells and vesper song —
The dreams where Joy and Peace enfold
The happy Argonauts and gold.

IN THE FOOTHILLS

HERE lie the wooded slopes that dreamers love,
Low, rolling hills, with purple peaks above,
And filled with hidden haunts and dusky dells,
Where Daphne roams and tender Fancy dwells.

Through shady thickets, dark with tangled vine,
Shy clusters of sweet, wilding berries shine;
And birds that through the leafy tree-tops dart
Wake answering music in the Dreamer's heart.

From some deep spring, hid in some silent nook,
Babbles across a field a bubbling brook,
Then through the cañon softly slides and slips
Where Echo stands with finger on her lips.

Across and in and out wind wavering trails
Among the glimmering glens and twilight dales,

15

And homeward herd-bells spice the dewy air
With thoughts of even-song and vesper prayer.

Here lies the Dreamer's Bethel — skies unfold,
Light ladders lean from lands of sunset gold,
Fair souls of fantasy descend to earth
And find within his happy heart a birth.

MORNING IN THE SIERRAS

ABOVE me rise the snowy peaks
    Where golden sunbeams gleam and quiver,
And far below, toward Golden Gate,
    O'er golden sand flows Yuba River.

Through crystal air the mountain mist
    Floats far beyond yon distant eagle,
And swift o'er crag and hill and vale
    Steps Morning, purple-robed and regal,

The while a breeze through cañons deep
    Sets all the tall tree-tops in motion,
Bearing a greeting to the pines
    From palms beside the Southern ocean.

SANTA CLARA VALLEY

(NEAR SAN JOSÉ)

To NORTH the waving tule skirts the bay,—
  No fairer bay e'er graced as fair a land,—
And o'er its ripples down the valley stray
  Soft zephyrs redolent of sea-swept sand.

To south a reach of meadow, farm, and lane,
  With peaceful herds and flocks in sweet repose,
Fair Ceres guarding fields of yellow grain,
  And cottages entwined with vine and rose.

To west Pomona's fair and fruitful land,
  Vineyard and orchard stretching mile on mile,
Where Learning, Health, and Peace, a chosen
    band,
  Bask in the golden light of Fortune's smile.

18

To east a purple peak with clouds impearled,
   A royal road that winding leads afar
Unto a Mecca of the Western world —
   The giant eye that scans the distant star.

Here in this land with milk and honey stored,
   O weary wanderer, stay thy pilgrim feet!
This is the land of promise and reward, —
   O rest thee here, and make life's sunset sweet!

DREAM VOICES

ALL day long sweet zephyr-fingers
    Touch the wind-harp's silver strings;
Bird and bee, and brook and blossom
    Understand the song it sings.

All night long star-voices whisper
    In the garden of the sky;
Spray and nest, and lake and lily
    Catch the echoes floating by.

But the busy world, unheeding,
    Hears no sweetness in the air;
Toil and care, and pain and sorrow
    Drown the voices everywhere.

Dreamers, only, stop to listen;
    Something says: "Be still and hark!"

Something, as the sound of ripples
    Kissing sea-sands in the dark,

Perfume as of rose still folded,
    Sound as of a brook at night,
Dusky shadows as of swallows
    Through the gloaming taking flight.

Thus the Dreamer hears, and hearing,
    Strives to set his voice in tune—
O the songs beyond his grasping,
    Heard beneath the mellow moon!—

Songs he fain would be repeating,
    Though the sweetness half be fled,—
Songs denied unto the Living,
    Are they granted to the Dead?

NAPA REVISITED

FAIR Valley!   Rich with memories,
    Filled to the brim with happy dreams,—
The dreams and memories that float
    Like flowers adown Life's sunny streams,
And, drifting through the harbor gate,
    Sail out across the sobbing sea,
Fading nor sinking, till they reach
    The haven-land, Eternity.

How fond, how dear, how memory-fraught
    Thy dells and dales, thy slopes and hills,
When daylight o'er, the yellow sun
    Fills all the sky with daffodils!
While dew-wet gardens, scented deep,
    Where roses with the violets vie,
Look up with sweetest smile to greet
    The angel gardens in the sky.

The very air is rife with dreams;
  The lute of love and lyre of light
Pour forth in never-ceasing strains
  Fair flowers of song that know no blight;
While poet-harps grown strangely dumb
  Awake in this enchanted land,
And melodies that glad the heart
  Fall from the Poet's trembling hand.

This is the *finis*, this the end
  Of search for Summer's lotos-land,
(Up from the south come cooling winds
  That lately kissed the sea-wet sand).
And I, with head bared to the breeze,
  Would fain find here my earthly rest,
Like to a weary child that lays
  Its head upon its mother's breast.

IN THE SANTA CRUZ MOUNTAINS

HIGH on a towering peak, I look
    Across the twilight bay;
Here Santa Cruz is nestling low,
    And there lies Monterey.

Far, far beyond, the breakers white
    Wreathe Cypress Point with snow,
Till dreams and darkness weave a veil
    O'er all the scene below.

The last low sheep-bell softly says
    "Good-night!" from some far fold,
And swiftly from the lighthouse dim
    Gleams forth a torch of gold.

WITH A CALENDAR

You know the promise that you made
Under the linden's leafy shade,
  When high above a lark sang clear,
And in my hand your hand you laid —
  You know, you said, "Some day next year!"
Accept this calendar, dear maid,
  'T will help you choose that day so dear!
Here all the seasons stand arrayed,
  Dark days, bright days, days far, days near;
Days when the corn is in the blade,
  Days when the corn is in the ear;
Days when green grass is in the glade,
  Days when the grass is brown and sere;
Days when sweet April's fingers braid
  A dewy wreath of smile and tear;
Days when moons of September fade
  In yellow glory on the mere —

In fact, I'm not at all afraid
    But that you'll find each day is here!
On which day shall Love's debt be paid?
You know the promise that you made
Under the linden's leafy shade!

AMONG THE BELMONT HILLS

Toward twilight-time we slowly pass
  Along a road whose winding turns
Are decked with dainty wildwood flowers,
  With trailing vines and graceful ferns;
Along a rail-fence runs a quail,
  A bluebird darts amid the trees,
And cow-bell echoes, dimly heard,
  Are wafted on the evening breeze.

Beside the edge of Crystal Lake
  We watch the June sun slowly fall,
While o'er the mountain creeps the fog,
  Like white smoke thro' the redwoods tall:
The waters, rippled by the wind,
  In pearl-tipped wavelets kiss the shore,
And Fancy catches dreamy hints
  Of hillside tale and lakeside lore.

Our way leads where moss-covered oak,
    Bright bay, and buckeye charm the glade,
While through the leaves the setting sun
    Weaves arabesques of shine and shade;
We pass the happy woodland homes
    That bask in San Mateo's smile,
Where sunny slope and dusky dell
    With dreamful rest the heart beguile.

Gray gloaming falls from darkening skies;
    Toward home we swiftly wend our way
As San Leandro's lights gleam out
    Across the blueness of the bay; —
Adieu to tranquil paths of peace!
    "Good-night!" we say to scenes so bright,
And down the cañon's starlit slope
    A woodbird softly calls "Good-night!"

APPROACH OF NIGHT

By the yellow in the sky,
    Night is nigh.

By the murk on mead and mere,
    Night is near.

By one faint star, pale and wan,
    Night comes on.

By the moon, so calm and clear,
    Night is here.

O'ERLOOKING THE SEA

(NEAR SKYLAND)

Across the silent silver sea
The silver moon looks wistfully;
High on the hills I stand and gaze
Across a reach of firs and bays
And redwoods tall with moss o'ergrown,
Filling the cañons dark and lone,
To where across the silver sea
The silver moon looks wistfully.

Above the silent silver sea
The silver stars beam tenderly;
From twilight-time till now a bell
Has twinkled in some distant dell,
And faint farm-sounds the still air fill
Blown in and out through vale and hill,

30

While far above the silver sea
The silver stars beam tenderly.

Across the silent silver sea
A silver sail drifts dreamily;
Up deep ravines the white fog runs —
Fair Amphitrite's hooded nuns, —
Hastening with reverent, holy air
To chant on land a midnight prayer —
While far across the silver sea
A silver sail drifts dreamily.

AN EASTER WISH

THE peace that lies in ocean depths
    Unstirred by storm and wind,
The peace that distant snow-white sails
    In sunset harbors find,
The peace of summer clouds astray
Be thine, this holy Easter Day.

The calm that wraps each leaf and spray
    In shadowy, flowery dells,
The calm that lingers in the air
    When cease the vesper bells,
The calm of lily-broidered ways
Be thine, this holiest of days.

The faith of Mary at the dawn
    Amid the garden dew,

The hope that blossomed in the hearts
   Of His disciples true,
The love that rolled the stone away
Be thine, this holy Easter Day.

CALIFORNIA

A SLEEPING beauty, hammock-swung,
    Beside the sunset sea,
And dowered with riches, wheat, and oil,
    Vineyard and orange-tree;
Her hand, her heart to that fair prince,
    Whose genius shall unfold
With rarest art her treasured tales
    Of life and love and gold.

AS I CAME DOWN MOUNT TAMALPAIS

As I came down Mount Tamalpais,
    To north the fair Sonoma Hills
Lay like a trembling thread of blue
    Beneath a sky of daffodils;
Through tules green a silver stream
    Ran south to meet the tranquil bay,
Whispering a dreamy, tender tale
    Of vales and valleys far away.

As I came down Mount Tamalpais,
    To south the city brightly shone,
Touched by the sunset's good-night kiss
    Across the golden ocean blown;
I saw its hills, its tapering masts,
    I almost heard its tramp and tread,
And saw against the sky the cross
    Which marks the City of the Dead.

As I came down Mount Tamalpais
   To east San Pablo's water lay,
Touched with a holy purple light,
   The benediction of the day;
No ripple on its twilight tide,
   No parting of its evening veil,
Save dimly in the far-off haze
   One dreamy, yellow sunset sail.

As I came down Mount Tamalpais,
   To west Heaven's gateway opened wide,
And through it, freighted with day-cares,
   The cloud-ships floated with the tide;
Then, silently through stilly air,
   Starlight flew down from Paradise,
Folded her silver wings and slept
   Upon the slopes of Tamalpais.

TWILIGHT IN LIVERMORE VALLEY

THE sun has set, and evening skies
    Begin, like rosebuds, to unfold,
While on the distant mountain top
    Still linger faint, stray gleams of gold,
Like kisses pressed by angel lips,
Or touches of God's finger-tips.

Like wreaths of purple violets,
    The hills around the valley lie,
And Mount Diablo's lofty peak
    Towers high into the twilight sky—
A stately sentinel it seems,
Guarding a land of dusk and dreams.

Up through the western mountain pass
    Night-breezes wander from the bay,

And whisper tender Dreamland tales
From sandy beaches far away,
Where drifting dream and beaming star
Clasp hands across the harbor bar.

Hesper unveils her lovely face;
I hear a star-voice downward fall
From some dim, distant lattice height
Above the far cerulean wall—
"Peace! Peace!" it calls, and all is calm
Beneath the night's o'ershadowing palm.

REVERIE

Comes the perfume of a rose
From the latticed garden close
Of a still, sequestered nook in Paradise,
  And the singing of a bird,
  Whose delicious notes are heard
In a bower that in some sweet elysium lies;
  Come the glimmers of a stream,
  Silver shining in a dream,
Silver chain that links the mountain to the
      sea,
  And the echoes vague, remote,
  That in tremulous fancy float
From that heaven where faint souls ever long
      to be —
  In the echo, in the gleam,
  In the song and scent I seem
Once again the old-time life to feel and know,

As fair fantasies of You,
Dim with dusk and damp with dew,
Cluster round the memory of long ago.

NIGHT IN THE REDWOODS

THE eyes that all day upward looked to feast
On sloping boughs, nor yet at twilight ceased,
Now see in trunk and branch, and leaf and spray
Diviner meanings than were felt by day —
The trunks that tower high, look up and out,
Like Faith above the undergrowth of Doubt;
The stately boughs, the sprays so far above,
Encompass Faith with arms of tender love;
The little leaves are servants fond and true,
Cup-bearers of the summer sun and dew.
These giant limbs, each spangled with a star,
Seem spirit-steps to heavenly lands afar,
And these wide-spreading arms, held high in air,
In quiet wait the answer to a prayer.
How still the scene! A century of calm
Lies wrapped within this night of blissful balm.

41

All still, save in the soul a breath, a call,
A thrill that holds the heart in solemn thrall,
One swelling pulse, one mighty undertone —
God's voice down through the redwood branches
    blown.

LAVENDER

A GATHERER of lavender,
    When all his work was o'er,
Fell fast asleep in slumber deep
    Upon his fragrant store;
And as the scent with fancy blent
    Charmed Sleep's fair silver streams,
This gatherer of lavender
    Went gathering fragrant dreams.

AT THE EDGE OF THE DAY

See Twilight standing on the brink
    That skirts the dark abyss of night;
The dew-wet roses in her hair
    Shed incense through the waning light,
Low in the west one lonely star
    Shines tremulous and white.

Across the far, dim edge of day,
    The task of morn and toil of noon
Slip noiselessly adown the tide
    With dusky shadows thickly strewn,
And o'er the lately purple hills
    Rises the yellow moon.

Go, Twilight, trembling on the verge
    'Twixt shadowy earth and shadowy air,

Fold peaceful hands on peaceful breast,
    Spread starlit wings and gently bear
To Heaven's gate a burden sweet —
    The World's low vesper prayer.

TREADING THE WINE-PRESS

NOCTURNE

ALONG the river bank I stray,
    About the time of dusk and dew;
The river ripples to the bay,
    My thoughts flow down the stream to you.

To you, upon the silver sands
    That girt the twilight-tinted sea,
From him who stands with outstretched hands,.
    Gazing to seaward wistfully.

Among the reeds the ripples sing
    A little song, half-sweet, half-sad,
While I, with tear-voiced whispering,
    Bid it for thy dear sake be glad.

I would that distance were not wide,
    That Fate might whisper low and sweet:.

" Set sail adown the trembling tide,
  And anchor at the loved one's feet! "

Fate standeth mute. And so my prayers,
  Like roses on the river's breast,
Float seaward; — may thy tears and cares
  Be soothed by sleep, and peace, and rest!

The hour grows late. Through meadows fair
  The river flows toward rest and thee
Meeting the sea-sand close to where
  A star is sinking to the sea.

THE THREE MISSIONS

THREE spirits met in upper realms of air,
    On earthly missions sent,
One robed in deepest sable, one in white,
    One white and sable blent.

The white-robed spirit broke the silence: "Lo!
    A child is born this night;
With joy I haste to place a snow-white soul
    Within its bosom white!"

"Sister," the gray-robed spirit whispered, "fast
    I follow after thee—
With cords of fate and mingled rose and rue,
    I weave a destiny!"

Up spake the third: "Hear ye! in one short hour
    Vanish both soul and spell,
I go to ring for mother and for child
    A funeral knell!"

REMEMBRANCE

A POET sings: "The winds of Fate
Sweep coldly through Life's open gate,
And leaf of laurel and of rose,
Each into Death's dark valley goes."
Yet sometimes up from that sad vale
To lifeward blows a timid gale
That wafts the scent of faded flowers
Into these lonesome lives of ours;
For just last night, when wearily
The gold moon sank into the sea,
And angel faces in the stars
Peered earthward through the silver bars,
I, looking out across the night,
Heard echoes from a far-off height,
A long-lost voice—my Mother dear!—
Singing in some dim, distant sphere,

REMEMBRANCE

While o'er my senses stole a scent
Of one white rose with jasmine blent,
The rose I laid upon her breast
The day she entered into rest.

A WATCH IN THE NIGHT

OPPRESSED by something in my troubled sleep,
   I, with a moan, awoke in deep despair—
Was it some daytime duty left undone,
   Or was it some forgotten kiss or prayer?

Something it was that made my pillow hard,
   Something my heart around or soul within—
I rose and looked across a night as dark,
   Yes, darker, than the fearful face of Sin!

Close, close at hand a midnight taper burned—
   I knew it for the lamp of my fierce foe;
I leaned far out—he could not help but hear:
   "Friend, I forgive thee every hurt and blow!"

A WATCH IN THE NIGHT

Down on my knees I fell and prayed for him
  Who wrong had done me many times and oft;
And as a star shone through a rifted cloud,
  I sought my couch and found the pillow soft!

ALONG A PATH IN PARADISE

ALONG a path in Paradise
   Two sad-eyed angels went;
At Heaven's gate they downward sped,
   On earthly missions sent.

That night two mortal enemies,
   In prayers of anguish born,
Vowed to the other pardon full
   Upon the morrow morn.

Along a path in Paradise
   Two angels passed, glad-eyed;
One bore a broken heart of hate,
   And one a heart of pride.

WEIGHTS AND MEASURES

THE heaviness of earth and air,
  The force of passing breeze,
The weight of crowns, and ships, and worlds—
  I wonder not at these.
I see the awful griefs and pains
  That faint souls undergo,
And wonder how the human heart
  Can bear such weight of woe.

The measurement of time and space,
  The depth of deepest seas,
The distance of the faintest star—
  I marvel not at these.
The measure that I marvel at,
  All measurement above,
Is this—the wondrous height and depth
  And length and breadth of Love!

58

THE JUDGMENT-BOOK

THE Book was opened! Men in wonder stood!
No record kept of wrong! It told of good!
Each deed of love! A Soul crept up in fright,
Then passed into the dark — his page was white!

THE ARROW

STRAIGHT from a mighty bow this truth is
    driven:
"They fail, and they alone, who have not
    striven."

Fly far, O shaft of light! all doubt redeem-
    ing;
Rouse men from dull despair and idle
    dreaming.

High Heaven's evangel be, gospel God-
    given:
"They fail, and they alone, who have not
    striven."

THE OLD YEAR

WHAT is the old year? 'T is a book
On which we backward sadly look,
Not willing quite to see it close—
For leaves of violet and rose
Within its heart are thickly strewn,
Marking Love's dawn and golden noon;
And turned-down pages, noting days
Dimly recalled through Memory's haze;
And tear-stained pages, too, that tell
Of starless nights and mournful knell
Of bells that toll through troubled air
The *De Profundis* of despair;
The laugh, the tear, the shine, the shade,
All 'twixt the covers gently laid,
No uncut leaves, no page unscanned—
Close it and lay it in God's hand.

THE FIRE OF FATE

THE fire of Fate blazed high one day
    And marked me for its prey;
With red-hot tongue it scorched my soul,
    And burned fair hopes away.

Across my heart a firebrand fell,
    As from the hearth of Hell,
And left a wound whose stinging smart
    No human tongue could tell.

Adown the weary Lane of Years,
    With sighs and anxious fears,
I bear my sin-seared heart and soul
    Unto the Gate of Tears,

Hoping that some fair angel's wing
    O'er me its shade will fling,

While to the Cross of Calvary
    With trembling hands I cling,

Praying that I His face may greet,
    Since through Fate's fiery heat
He too did pass, with riven side
    And piercéd hands and feet.

GHOSTS

THREE ghosts there are that haunt the heart
    Whate'er the hour may be—
The ghost called Life, the ghost called Death,
    The ghost called Memory.

SORROW AND SOLACE

An awful grief o'erwhelmed my soul;
　　From friend and priest I fled —
I scorned their speech, refused relief;
　　Would not be comforted.

An angel, softly whispering "Peace!"
　　Crept closely to my side;
But no — my wild, rebellious pain
　　Would not be pacified.

But O, the spell, so strange, so sweet,
　　Between my heart and thine,
That soothed my woe the moment that
　　Your eyes and lips met mine!

A GOLDEN DAY

A SUN of suns crept up to greet
    A day from all days set apart
A golden glow o'er all the world,
    A golden hope within my heart;
A hope that blossomed like a flower,
    As morn expanded into noon,
Then faded in the twilight dim,
    And died beneath the yellow moon.

O, not until the morrow's sun
    Proclaimed my day and night far fled,
Could I believe that Faith was false,
    That Love was cold and Hope lay dead.
And yet how fair and bright it shone,
    My golden Hope that turned to clay! —
Tho' years have passed, down Life's gray sky
    Still shines my golden yesterday.

A SONG OF TRIUMPH

To-DAY I sing a victor-strain,
   A hymn of praise,—
A canticle of joyous sound
   I upward raise.

From boughs that thickly overhang
   The battle-field,
I pluck fair laurel leaves with which
   To deck my shield.

My spear and helmet, too, I twine
   With leaves of bay,
In token of my victory
   In furious fray

Yet no man's blood bestains my mail,
   And, what is best,

No ghastly face nor dying moan
    Disturbs my rest.

To-day, between Heaven's holy hill
    And Hell's dark pit,
I met a Sin that tempted me,
    And conquered it.

LOVE'S LOYALTY

I OFFERED you a goblet filled
    With wine so richly red;
Deep in my soul I pledged a toast:
    "The day on which we wed!"

You drank the wine, and straightway dashed
    The goblet at my feet;
With mocking laugh that echoes yet,
    You sought the crowded street.

And yet I cannot curse your name,
    Forget your face or form,
While to my breast I press the glass
    Touched by your fingers warm!

I wooed you for my bonnie bride;
    You gave your heart and hand,
And forth we wandered arm in arm
    Across the twilight-land.

III

I sang for you one starless night—
    My tears fell like the rain;
You bade me sing "Abide with me,"—
    I did not end the strain!
You closed your eyes, and lo! your ears
    With angel music rang.
I wonder if you e'er recall
    The earthly songs I sang.

A POET'S EPITAPH

A LIFE with day-dreams and night visions
        fraught;—
But oh, the good these dreams and visions
        wrought!

ANTE MORTEM

SPARE not thy hand when approbation giving,
    Nor hold thy tongue till life away has sped —
A single word of praise unto the Living
    Is worth a panegyric on the Dead.

THE SONGS I SANG FOR YOU

I

I SANG for you one early morn
    When leaves with dew were wet;
Tho' years have passed, that simple song
    Rings in my memory yet.
I crowned you with a diadem
    Of blossoms fair and sweet,—
You were my little Queen of Flowers;
    I lay low at your feet.

II

I sang for you one afternoon—
    A bird sang overhead;
"Your song is far the sweeter song,"—
    Those were the words you said.

I wooed you for my bonnie bride;
   You gave your heart and hand,
And forth we wandered arm in arm
   Across the twilight-land.

III

I sang for you one starless night—
   My tears fell like the rain;
You bade me sing "Abide with me,"—
   I did not end the strain!
You closed your eyes, and lo! your ears
   With angel music rang.
I wonder if you e'er recall
   The earthly songs I sang.

74

A POET'S EPITAPH

A LIFE with day-dreams and night visions
    fraught; —
But oh, the good these dreams and visions
    wrought!

LOVE AND DOUBT

TO-DAY into my heart of hearts
    There crept a tiny Doubt;
There was no room for Love and it —
    So Love was driven out.

And oh, to think how sure I was
    Last night our love was true,
And that to-day this little Doubt
    Had bidden Love adieu!

"No room within for Love and Doubt,"
    I heard my sad heart say;
And, looking in your eyes, I knew
    That Doubt had come to stay!

O for two narrow graves of grief,
   That we might lie therein!
My heart with all its weight of woe,
   Your heart with all its sin.

STUBBLE

Ghost of the vanished days when April dew
　　Lay on the fresh, sweet-scented fields;
Naught but the memory of long ago
　　Your deathly fragrance yields.

Sad souvenir of Springtime's sapphire blue,
　　Dim dreamer of the May-time air,
To-day both you and I look back and say:
　　"Past days — how very fair!"

A DREAM OF DEATH

DEATH came to me and said: "One day
   Is given thee to live;
Ask what thou wilt for thy last hour
   And I that gift will give."

I did not dare to ask that I
   Might claim a farewell kiss;
I could not bear to see thy face
   In such an hour as this!

"Grant me, O Death! a simple boon,
   All other gifts above,—
Grant me sweet sleep, and let me die
   Dreaming of her I love!"

WITH LAUGH AND SONG

AL FRESCO

I

COME!   No longer wander this way,
   Leave the dusty road beneath us;
Let us seek a purer bliss-way,
   Where no thorns of earth shall wreathe us!
Down the path a bevy passes,
   Children with their luncheon-pails,
Mirth like flute-notes in the grasses,
   Viol-notes from virgin vales!
Woo us not, O Youth, in May-time!
   We have known Life's rocks and billows,
Sun-tents now our rest by daytime,
   Star-shine round our peaceful pillows!
Farewell now to cares and sorrows;
   We are princes, priests, and kings,
Pressing toward the glad to-morrows
   Of our woodland wanderings!

Up the steep slope, sun-rejoicing,
  Diademed with leafy laurel,—
Here's a song that needs no voicing,
  Here's a tale that points no moral!
Canticle and hymn and psalter,
  Graced with all the greenwood arts,
Framed by lips that never falter,
  Wafted to world-weary hearts!

II

Low lights mid the buckeyes playing,
  Guess at haunt of faun and dryad;
Sea-winds vesper Aves saying,
  Soothe the wood-dove's jeremiad;
Purple sunset shallops sailing
  To the ports on Evening's shore;
Weird and mystic shadows veiling
  Chaparral and sycamore.
Hush!   Adown ravines and hollows
  Echo wanders, dreamy-sandaled.

Look!   A flight of home-bound swallows
    Flecks the sky by Twilight candled.
Come!   Far in the dusky forest,
    Let us build a pyre to Pan!
All that grieved us, made us sorest,
    All that bore a curse or ban,
In Oblivion's volume file them —
    Stinging gibe or cruel jeering —
Gayly on the altar pile them —
    Critic's frown and cynic's sneering!
See!   The flames leap high and higher, —
    Vanish pains and wounds and scars!
Let us sleep with feet to fire,
    Backs to earth, and eyes to stars!

A CHAT WITH DICK

A chat with Dick! When winds are high,
And pelting rains rush rudely by,
    Or else in sweeter scenes than these,
    When stars peep through the locust-trees,
And Summer winds are soft and shy!

Let men for gold and silver vie,
Let men for laurels live and die,—
    I 'll choose for my part, if you please,
        A chat with Dick!

O Fortune! drain my rivers dry,
Send blinding tears, and cloud my sky;
    Take happiness and wealth and ease;
    Lock Pleasure's doors and lose the keys,—
All this, and more, but don't deny
        A chat with Dick!

TOLD TO A CHILD

Do you know the fairy measure—
Lilting measure that they dance to
When the moon is in the crescent
    And the busy world is still,—
When each sprite and fay and fairy
Steps from out the rose and lily
And goes tripping to the woodland
    Just behind the purple hill?

Have you seen the pearls and laces,
And the fans bedecked with jewels?
Have you caught the sheen of diamonds
    And the gowns so rich and rare,
As the fairies swing and circle
Round a harebell hung with glow-worms,
While the crickets in the heather
    Sing a glad and joyous air?

Have you heard the happy laughter
When the fairy dance is over
And the golden moon is sinking
   In a sea of amber dye?
Have you heard the "Good-night" wafted
From the roses and the lilies?
Have you heard the good-night kisses
   Blown across the shadowy sky?

Is it so — you have not seen them?
Can it be you have not heard them —
Never caught the fairy measure
   On a starlit Summer night?
And you say there are no fairies?
And you don't believe my story?
Well!   It must be that I dreamed it
   'Neath the new moon's crescent light!

DOWN THE LANE

FAR down the lane as eye can reach,
  The hedges are aglow
With roses red and roses pink
  And roses white as snow;
For 't is the rose-month, queen of months,
  June odors in the air,
And Phyllis wanders down the lane
  With roses in her hair

And I — I am a little bird
  Perched on an alder spray;
I look across the field and see
  Some one not far away:
I watch them both, till at the stile
  They meet — and then think best
To turn my head away and sing,
  And let you guess the rest!

BOATMAN'S SONG

FLY, fly my boat, across the sea!
　The sun is on the wane,
　The last beams linger wistfully
　　Upon the steeple vane—
The reapers are leaving the fields of grain,
And a face is pressed on the window-pane.

Fly, fly my boat, across the sea!
　Dim shadows veil the strand,
　And twilight hues glide hazily
　　Across the sea and sand, —
But I see a form on the nearing land,
Looking this way with a shading hand.

Fly, fly my boat, across the sea!
　Leave wind and wave and roar;

The time has come for you and me
     To lay aside the oar—
There is rest for thee on the peaceful shore,
And a kiss for me at the open door.

ROSITA

I

HERE'S a song of sweet Rosita,
　　She is the fairest!
Of the maidens in the village
　　She is the queen!
When she wanders in the garden,
　　'Mid all the flowers,
She's the sweetest and the rarest rose
　　That ever was seen!
　　　　In the dancing,
　　　　So entrancing,
　　　　When, so sadly,
　　　　Then, so gladly,
　　Castanet and gay guitar
　　Keep time for tripping feet—

Oh,
Of the charms of sweet Rosita,
    I could be singing
From the dawn of golden morning
    Till day-beams depart!
But e'en then her charms I could not
    One half be telling —
Little Rose of love and beauty,
    The queen of my heart!

II

Lovely eyes has my Rosita
    And jet-black tresses;
And her voice!   It is the sweetest
    That ever was heard!
Oft at eve I seek her cottage,
    Then I call softly;
Quickly down the little garden path,
    She flies like a bird!

93

In the gloaming,
Sweetly roaming,
Where the lime-trees
Scent the night-breeze,—
How I love to hear her sing
The songs of sunny Spain!
Oh,
Of the charms of sweet Rosita,
I could be singing
From the dawn of golden morning
Till day-beams depart!
But e'en then her charms I could not
One half be telling—
Little Rose of love and beauty,
The queen of my heart!

MY HEART TO THEE IS SINGING

I

WHEN dew bediamonds leaf and spray,
   And sprinkles reeds and sedges,
And all the east a ruby glows,
   With opals round the edges;
When violets ope their dreamy eyes
   And larks are skyward winging,
The while my thoughts fly o'er the sea,
   My heart to thee is singing:

   O Love, tho' Fate part hands and lips,
     And thou dost shine afar;
   From dawn to dusk thou art my sun,
     From dusk to dawn my star!

II

When birds and roses fall asleep
    Amid the hawthorn hedges;
When vales grow dark and hills grow blue,
    With gold and crimson edges;
When one pale star unveils its face,
    And vesper bells are ringing,
The while my thoughts fly o'er the sea,
    My heart to thee is singing:

    O Love, tho' Fate part hands and lips,
        And thou dost shine afar,
    From dawn to dusk thou art my sun,
        From dusk to dawn my star!

RECONCILIATION

I

I SOMETIMES wonder when and how
    You will come back to me—
Across what stretch of burning sand,
    Across what sobbing sea—
What word will break the silence long
    That now sweet speech denies,
And what will be the tale that each
    Reads in the other's eyes.

II

Will floods of sunshine, golden fair,
    Across our pathway flow,
Or will our souls in rapture meet
    Beneath the starlight's glow?

Will flowers bloom, birds sweetly sing,
    To welcome in the day,
Or will dead leaves be blown across
    A sky of tearful gray?

III

Let it be soon!   Come as it may,
    Enough there is of pain
Without the added weight of woe,
    If love like ours were slain.
Come back to life and hope and joy—
    These arms are open wide!
Come back and find our early love,
    Thorn-crowned, but sanctified!

TO A SINGER

Thou hast the gift of gifts!   Go seek for bliss
   In far, strange lands, through long and weary
        years,
Thou wilt not find a greater boon than this—
   The power to move thy listeners to tears.

MY LOVE FOR YOU

I

HARD it is to tell when love begins —
All the birds are singing, when love begins;
    Hearts that find the treasure
    Know no bound or measure,
    Life is naught but pleasure,
      When love begins!
I know a love that has no beginning or ending,
Like April fair, sunshine and shadow blending;
Chaste as the snow and pure as the heavenly blue,
No other love can ever compare with my love
      for you!

II

Easy 't is to tell when love is o'er —
Birds are no more singing when love is o'er;

Hearts that lose the treasure
Know full well its measure,
Life hath naught of pleasure,
When love is o'er!
I know a love that has no beginning or ending;
Like April fair, sunshine and shadow blending;
Chaste as the snow and pure as the heavenly blue,
No other love can ever compare with my love
for you!

THE TEMPLE SCENE IN "AIDA"

PRAISE, incense, prayer, and deepest adoration,
  (Pink water-lilies on the mystic Nile,)
Uplifted hands and eyes and incantation,
  (Deserted deserts, stretching mile on mile).

Weird music from the inner temple rising,
  (A camel dark against a distant sky,)
The altar spread for holy sacrificing,
  (An Afric wind that passes with a sigh).

The notes of harp and timbrel, sounds entrancing,
  (A light gazelle, by palm-trees halfway hid,)
The priestesses in slow and solemn dancing,
  (A dim, white moon above a pyramid).

Loud parting chorus to the mighty Isis,
    (A blood-red sun that slowly seaward sinks,)
The air deep-filled with mystery and spices,
    (Egyptian darkness and the silent Sphinx).

TIES

THE dawn-light heeds the call of Day,
    Hope wreathes the prison bars,
Dream-angels watch where children pray,
    And Twilight woos the stars.

The river seeks the silvery foam,
    Sea-ripples kiss the sand,
And evening sails fly swiftly home
    To greet a beckoning hand.

And yet, dear one, this happy thought
    Pervades the song I sing,
Like some sweet benediction caught
    From some bright seraph's wing—

TIES

The strongest ties that Nature knows,
    I care not what they be,
Are but as naught compared with those
    Which bind my heart to thee!

TO HAZEL

YES, Hazel, I'm in love with you,—
 E'en you the fact will not dispute;
Else why should Cupid bid me sing
 The while he strikes his soft-toned lute?
And you love me? Why should I ask?
 Although your lips you close —
The south wind does not need to speak
 To tell it loves the rose!

O Hazel dear! this day is blest!
 The light of your blue eyes and mine
Has blended in a fadeless star
 No other star shall e'er outshine;
Your smile has poured a golden flood
 Of sunshine on my heart,
And never will our warm hand-clasp
 From memory depart!

TO HAZEL

Can I forget your eyes, your smile,
    The pressure of your tiny hand?
No!   Sooner bird forget its mate,
    Or sea forget the silver sand!
And yet I should not be surprised
    To see your love grow cold—
(Don't judge her harshly, reader, for
    She's only nine months old!)

A DREAM TALE

THE dim dream-gatherers one night
    Drew near my bed;
I felt them pass their dew-wet hands
    Across my head.
I caught the smell of salt sea brine;
    I heard them say:
"White sails and precious freight be thine!"
    Then it was day.

I wondered what the dream could mean —
    What ship?   What freight?
With eager eyes, I sat and watched
    The harbor gate;
At golden noon that very day
    My dream came true —
Love's white-winged ship sailed up the bay
    And brought me You!

PIANO SOLO

As UP and down the ivory keys
    Her slender fingers go,
I hear the rustle of a breeze,
    I hear a brooklet faintly flow —
As up and down the ivory keys
    Her slender fingers go.

As up and down her fingers go
    Across the ivory keys,
I hear a whisper, soft and low,
    Like hum of honey-laden bees —
As up and down her fingers go
    Across the ivory keys.

As up and down the ivory keys
    Her slender fingers go,

I see white sails on Summer seas,
    Touched by the sunset's golden glow —
As up and down the ivory keys
    Her slender fingers go.

As up and down her fingers go
    Across the ivory keys,
Dim dreams glide gently to and fro,
    Like night-winds 'mid the poplar trees —
As up and down her fingers go
    Across the ivory keys.

As up and down the ivory keys
    Her slender fingers go,
Sweet Slumber, wooed by sounds like these,
    Presses my weary eyelids low —
As up and down the ivory keys
    Her slender fingers go.

TO MY BLOTTING–PAD

My blotting-pad!   Dear friend, to thee
I owe the boon of sympathy!
For in this world where taunt and jeer
Ring loudly on the Dreamer's ear,
And where the Rhymester's tuneful art
Is trampled in the busy mart,
Where verse and song and flowery speech
Lie stranded on Fate's barren beach—
From out the chaos of despair
Thou steppest forth with friendly air,
And as the thoughts flow from the pen,
Before they reach the eyes of men,
Thou dost bestow on them and this
The benediction of a kiss!

THE WILD GRASS

I HEARD the wild grass, grieving, sigh
Because the reapers passed it by:
"For me no sickle's happy whirr,
No jocund song of harvester,
No high-heaped wains that plenty bring,
No joys of autumn garnering."
" But if thou hadst not grown," I said,
" No sheep would on the hills have fed;
And if no sheep had come this way,
No shepherd would have piped his lay;
And if no lay sweet love confess,
There surely were no shepherdess;
And if no shepherdess forlorn,
The kiss and vow had ne'er been born!"
A glad thrill thro' the dry grass spread:
" I wish them joy," it softly said.

TO THE MOON

O DREAM-BOAT! gliding through the starry sea,
Touching with silver light the willow-tree
 That waves in silence o'er my sweetheart's cot,
Seek not too soon thy haven o'er the hill,
But fondly creep across her window-sill,
 And enter in where I, alas, dare not!

Let one dear ray fall on her bosom white,
While from my mandolin with fingers light
 I draw a tender tune oft heard by thee —
Not loud enough her slumber soft to break,
And yet just clear and sweet enough to make
 Her dreaming heart dream one sweet dream
  of me!

YOU

"The chief want in life is somebody who shall make us do the best we can."—EMERSON.

A FLASH! You came into my life,
  And lo, adown the years
Rainbows of promise stretched across
  The sky grown gray with tears;
By day you were my sun of gold,
  By night my silver moon —
I could not from the Father's hands
  Have asked a greater boon!

Life's turbid stream grew calm and clear,
  The cold winds sank to rest,
Hand-clasped with you, no bitter pain
  Found dwelling in my breast;
I did not dread Life's care and toil —
  Your love dispelled all gloom,—

And now on graves of buried hopes
    The sweetest violets bloom.

My every breath and every thought
    Were pure because of you —
I had not dreamed that Heaven could be
    So close to mortal view;
My hands and feet were swift to do
    The good that near them lay,
And in my heart throughout the year
    The joy-bird sang each day.

A flash! You passed out of my life —
    No, no; your spirit still
Is sun and moon and guiding star
    Through every cloud and ill;
As down the rainbowed years I go,
    You still are at my side,
And some day I shall stand with you
    Among the glorified.

THREE SONGS OF LOVE

Sing no sad song of bygone days,
Now veiled in memory's tearful haze;
I would forget the hopes and fears
That filled with pain the former years;
Those flowers are dead, those suns have set,
Those joys have changed to vague regret;
The love I crave along life's way
Is not the love of yesterday.

Sing no blithe song of time and tide
That in some heavenly sphere abide;
Paint no fair scene of coming bliss
In tender look, hand-clasp, and kiss;
Those words sound vain in ears like mine;
Suns may not rise, stars fail to shine,
Birds may not sing in boughs above—
Oh, sing not of to-morrow's love!

Sing me a song, a happy song,
Full-voiced, with cadence rich and strong;
Gather no notes from olden themes,
Nor from the mystic land of dreams;
But sing in ringing rune and rhyme
The rapture of the present time.
Go, past and future—sing, I pray,
Of love that lives and loves to-day!

MABEL'S EYES

Mabel's eyes are oh, so blue!
Just like twin stars dipped in dew,
Colored with the tint one gets
Only from Spring violets!
Long ago, at love's sweet birth,
First I learned their precious worth,
And a chart for seas and skies
Fashioned out of Mabel's eyes.

Mabel's eyes were made to woo —
She can utilize them, too!
Bid me knight and courtier be,
Make a very slave of me!
Adoration they compel —
It would never do to tell
Everything that I surmise
Gazing into Mabel's eyes!

Mabel's eyes are oh, so true!
Never old and never new!
Beacon lights are they to me
Cruising on Life's troubled sea;
Rock and reef and storm and wind
All are quickly left behind,
Sailing toward the port I prize —
Port of Love, in Mabel's eyes!